BRAIN-IN-A-BOX

STEVE MATTHEWS
Illustrated by Mark Wilson

sundance

A Haights Cross Communications Company

Published by
Sundance Publishing
234 Taylor Street
Littleton, MA 01460

Copyright © text Steve Matthews
Copyright © illustrations Mark Wilson
Project commissioned and managed by
Lorraine Bambrough-Kelly, The Writer's Style
Designed by Cath Lindsey/design rescue

First published 1998 by
Addison Wesley Longman Australia Pty Limited
95 Coventry Street
South Melbourne 3205 Australia
Exclusive United States Distribution: Sundance Publishing

ISBN 0-7608-3284-6

CONTENTS

To my wife Lorraine — for putting up with me!

CHAPTER 1

THE MAGIC WASHING MACHINE

"Come on, get to sleep," Mom said, as she tucked Tom into bed. "Tomorrow's a big day for you. You're going on a field trip at school, remember?"

"Sure I do, Mom—to the Science Museum," Tom said. For once he didn't mind going to bed on time. He loved field trips, and the Science Museum was his idea of the perfect trip.

Like most kids, Tom always asked a lot of questions. He remembered a time when he was younger and had asked, "Mom, how do washing machines work?"

"Well," Mom had replied thoughtfully, "you put the laundry in the hole in the top, shut the lid, switch it on, and the clothes twirl around and around in the water and come out clean."

"Like magic?" Tom had asked.

"It's not really magic, no," Mom had replied.

"Well, I've invented a magic washing machine!" Tom said proudly.

He dragged Mom down the hallway to inspect his invention.

"You put the wash in here," he said, dropping some clothes in through the hole in the top.

"Then you close the lid and pull this handle on the side," he continued.

"Open the lid again and, presto!"

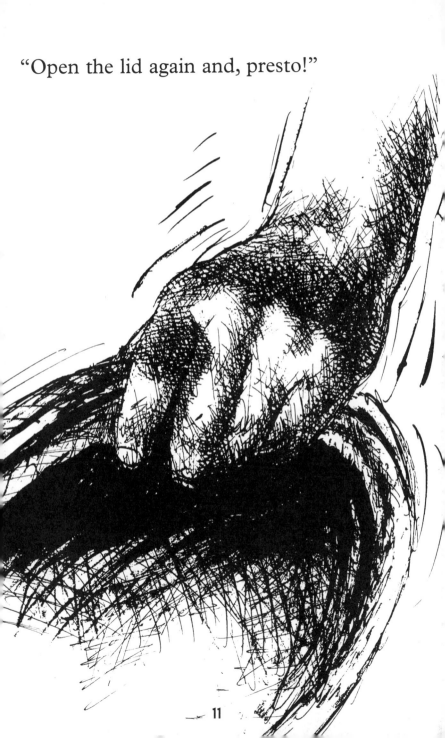

Tom and Mom peered inside. The clothes had disappeared.

"Perhaps it would work better if you didn't use the toilet," Mom said patiently.

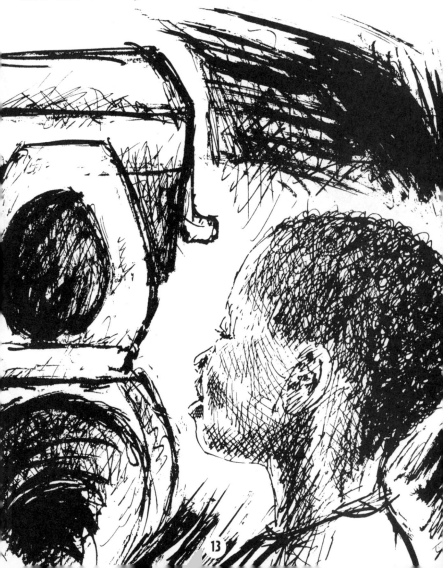

Tom smiled to himself sleepily, as he recalled his magic washing machine . . .

It was not long before Tom was sound asleep, dreaming of projects and experiments, and of all the wonders in the Science Museum.

CHAPTER 2

WHAT DO YOU MEAN —A BRAIN?

"What does this machine do?" Tom asked the museum guide.

"It makes electricity," she answered.

"How?" Tom asked.

"Well," the guide began, "this wheel turns

around, and the electricity is generated here." She pointed to a huge chrome ball.

"When you touch the ball, the electricity travels up your arm and through your body and makes your hair stand on end!"

Tom tried it. He looked weird with his hair
all pointy. "Excellent!" he yelled.

"And what about this?"

"This is an earthquake machine. You stand on the plate on the floor and it rattles and shakes, so you know what an earthquake feels like."

Tom rushed here and there, asking
questions, trying experiments, and starting,
pushing, and holding gadgets. He even
went to the museum gift shop and spent
the money Mom had given him that
morning.

"What did you buy?" Mom asked when he got home.

"A brain!" Tom said proudly.

"What do you mean, *a brain?*"

"A Brain-in-a-Box," Tom replied, handing it to his mother.

She examined it closely. It was a clear plastic box with a small, gray rubber brain that grew if you put water in with it. It was called Brain-in-a-Box. When it had grown, kids could examine it to see what a real brain looked like.

Mom helped Tom fill the brain's plastic box with water. She placed it by his bed for him to study. Imagine his surprise when it had grown to three times its size by the next day!

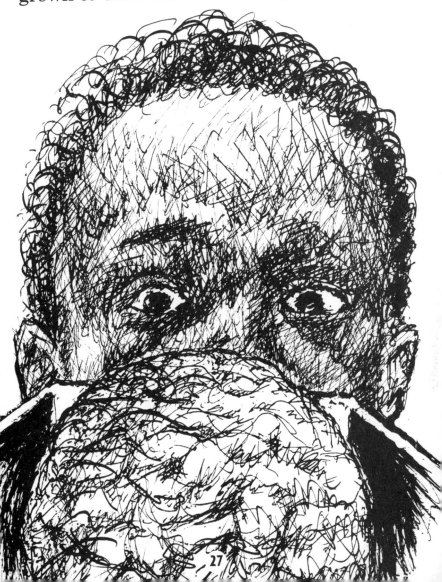

"How did the trip to the museum go, Tom?" Dad asked, as he appeared at the bedroom door.

"Great," Tom replied.

"I suppose you asked a million questions."

"Sure did!" Tom said brightly.

"You'll be telling us how car engines work next, eh?" Dad said, grinning.

"By internal combustion," Tom replied casually.

"What? Oh, right," Dad said, as he rushed off to finish getting ready for work.

Tom finished his breakfast. He wiped some sticky jam from his face with the back of his hand and wandered back to his room.

Tom looked at the Brain-in-a-Box. It lay there, gray and silent. He picked up the box, slipped it into his schoolbag, and rushed off to school.

CHAPTER 3

TWO BRAINS ARE BETTER THAN ONE

Tom was walking past the teachers' room on his way to class when he saw Mr. Washington, the English teacher, trying to do a crossword puzzle.

"Hmmm," Mr. Washington said out loud, "I need another word for *bulge*."

"Try *protuberance*," Tom said casually.

"What? What was that you said?"

"*Protuberance*, sir. It means the same as *bulge*," Tom explained.

"How did you know that? You're only in third grade."

"It was just a lucky guess," Tom said, shrugging.

"How about this?" Mr. Washington asked, scanning the crossword puzzle. "Give me another word for *disagreement*."

Tom hesitated for a moment, then said, "*Conflict*, sir. Or you could use *dispute*."

Mr. Washington stood up and stared at Tom for a moment. Everyone in the teachers' room stared at him. And the kids in the hallway stared, too.

Tom felt himself go red. He felt very self-conscious. It was embarrassing being so clever.

He patted his schoolbag, and a tingle of electricity shot through him. Inside the bag was the Brain-in-a-Box.

Tom seemed to know the answer to every question that day. Even the hardest problems in math were easy for him. There was nothing he didn't know. Word soon got around the school that Tom was a genius!

CHAPTER 4

BRAIN SQUEEZE

As he sat alone in his bedroom that night, Tom stared at the Brain-in-a-Box. It seemed to be moving, and it was fully grown. It glowed and gave off a humming noise, like a small electric motor.

What was it that was so odd about the brain? How come, since he had bought it, he knew all the answers to everything?

"Because you are the chosen one," a voice suddenly said. "Yes, that's right, it's me speaking. The Brain-in-a-Box."

Tom sat upright, startled by the voice.

"Don't be scared, Tom," said the Brain. "Together we will be famous. One day we will rule the world. But first you have to take me out of this box. Then we can begin the takeover."

"But I'm just a kid," Tom said. "I don't want to rule the world."

"Yes, you do," yelled the Brain. "We will discover things together. Stuff you have never even dreamed of. Open the box, Tom, and take me out. We will be together forever."

"No way, you horrible brain!" Tom yelled. "You stay right where you are. Leave me alone!"

He jumped off the bed, but as he moved to get away, he accidentally knocked the Brain-in-a-Box onto the floor.

The brain lay on the carpet, a lump of gray staring up at him.

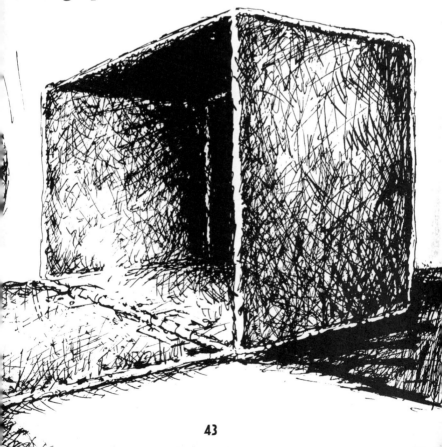

As Tom ran toward the door, the brain began to jiggle. Then it sprang after Tom.

"Get away!" Tom yelled. He batted the brain down and raced out of the room—pulling the door behind him.

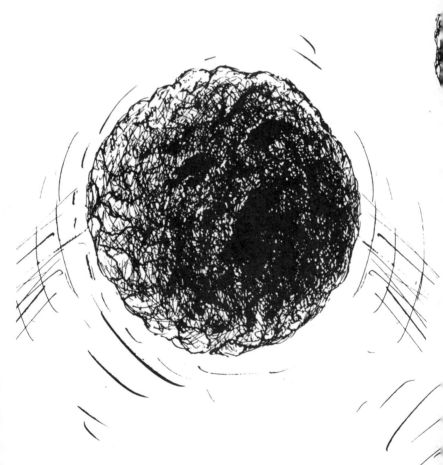

He could still hear the brain ranting and roaring inside the room.

"You little fool! I am the brain. If you help me, we can rule the world, and you can have everything you ever wanted. Now LET ME OUT!!!"

CHAPTER 5

ATTACK OF THE BRAIN

Tom gasped!

The door had swung open, and the brain was flying towards him.

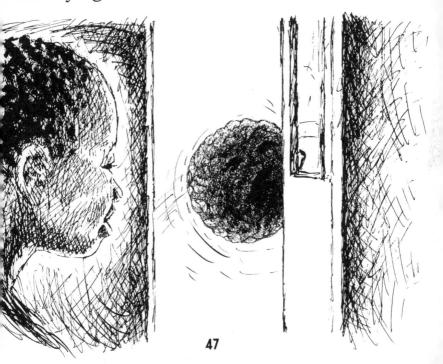

He yelled louder and louder.

"Help, save me! Mom, Dad, save me . . .
Help!"

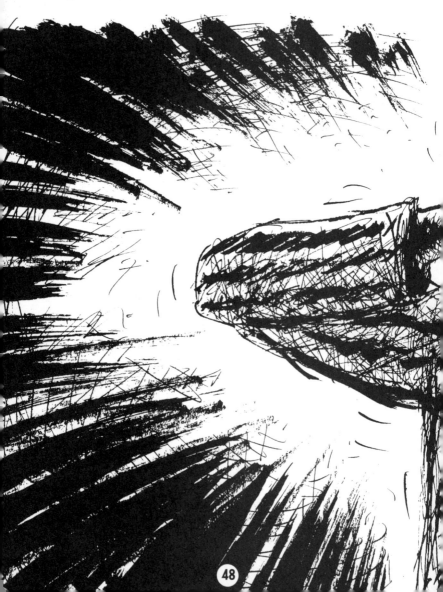

Mom burst into the room. "Tom! Tom! What's the matter?" she yelled, shaking him wildly. "Wake up, Tom, wake up!"

"The Brain-in-a-Box! It's out to get me—it wants to rule the world! Help me, Mom, help me!"

"What brain in what box? What's going on, Tom? Come on, you have to get up. You're going to the Science Museum today."

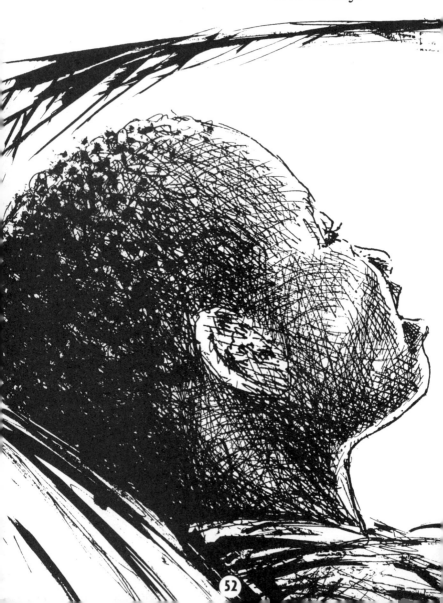

"Today? What do you mean I'm going today?" he asked. "Didn't I go just a few days ago?"

"I don't know what you are talking about, Tom. You must have been dreaming or something . . ."

CHAPTER 6

JUST ADD WATER

So it had all been a bad dream. Thank goodness! Tom was relieved to find out that the terrible adventure with the brain had just been a nightmare. Now he had the real trip to look forward to!

The Science Museum was everything Tom
had ever imagined it would be, and more.
So many things to see. So many answers to
so many questions. By the end of the day
he was exhausted.

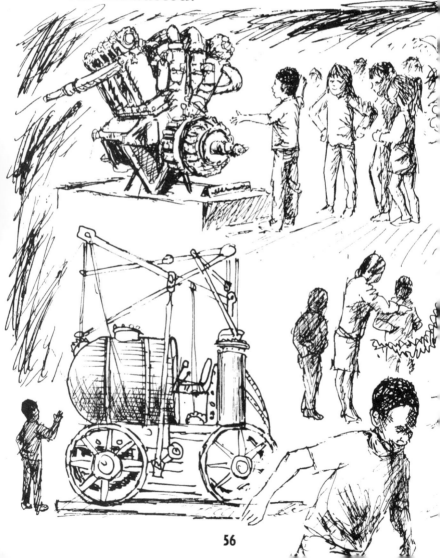

"Come on, class," the teacher yelled. "The bus leaves in ten minutes. We've got just enough time for a quick visit to the gift shop and then we have to go."

Tom wandered up and down the aisles, looking at the shelves. Everything you could think of was there — pencils, pens, rulers, and postcards. Just as he was about to go, he heard someone call to him.

"Tom . . . psssttt . . . Tom, over here . . ."

He looked around, but he seemed to be the only person there—apart from the sales clerk who was busy stacking the shelves at the other end of the shop.

Then he heard the voice again.

"Tom, over here, on the bottom shelf."

The voice was coming from the next aisle.

He walked over to the shelf where the voice came from and bent down to examine a small package. He turned it over and read the printing: BRAIN-IN-A-BOX ~ JUST ADD WATER.

He carefully opened the lid. Inside was a small, gray rubber brain.

"Tom." It was that voice again, the brain's voice. "Buy me, Tom. Take me home with you. Together we can rule the world!"

ABOUT THE AUTHOR

Steve Matthews

Steve Matthews, who was born in England in 1953, began writing children's stories in 1994. He lives in a secluded house in New South Wales, Australia, with his wife, two of his three children (hello!), two dogs (woof woof!), and four mischievous chickens (cluck cluck!).

ABOUT THE ILLUSTRATOR

Mark Wilson

Mark was born in Melbourne, Australia, and was encouraged to draw very early in his life by his father (a photographer) and his mother (a painter).

Mark studied painting and mural design in the 1970's. When he wasn't busy pretending to be a rock drummer, he worked in book and magazine design and illustration.

When Mark paints, he works in acrylics or oils and often paints with anything within reach, including pieces of cardboard, twigs, or leaves. He draws with pencils and also likes working in pen and ink. Mark has illustrated many children's books.